Ragged Island Mysteries™

D0925994

Watching Josh

by Deborah Eaton

**Wright Group
McGraw-Hill**

With thanks to Jennifer for the gifts of one convict, one babysitter, and a ton of trust; and to the Squares, who proved they are true friends with an amazing tolerance for whining

Watching Josh
Text copyright © Deborah Eaton
Illustrations copyright © Wright Group/McGraw-Hill
Illustrations by Taylor Bruce

Ragged Island Mysteries™ is a trademark of The McGraw-Hill Companies, Inc.

Wright Group/McGraw-Hill
19201 120th Avenue NE, Suite 100
Bothell, WA 98011
www.WrightGroup.com

Printed in the United States of America

10 9 8 7 6 5 4 3

ISBN: 0-322-01583-9
ISBN: 0-322-01651-7 (6-pack)

Jinx

Allie

Liz

Drew

Puffin

CONTENTS

1
AHOY, MARY POPPINS!

"Hold it right there! I've got a bomb. I'll blow up this whole island."

"Well, hurry up and do it, then," said Drew. "My arm's getting tired holding this boat." He tossed his backpack into the battered rowboat.

"Okay," said Josh. The six-year-old was squatting on the sand, an action figure clutched in each hand. "But I can't REALLY drop the bomb because then the bad guy would win."

He smacked the two plastic men together. "Take that!" he whispered. "And that! ARRRGH!"

Then he stuffed the toys in his pockets. He let Drew lift him into the boat.

A few islanders still left their rowboats here all year, anchored in the sand at the edge of the tide. They didn't seem to mind if kids played in them. Drew pushed this one into the water and jumped in himself. The anchor rope kept the boat close to the beach.

Josh ran from side to side. The old boat tipped wildly. Drew grabbed for the rail. "And I thought baby-sitting for a couple of hours a day after school would be easy," he thought.

"Here you go, you terror." He handed Josh a stick hung with string and a fishing hook. Josh grinned. A dimple made a big dent in each cheek. His thick, brown hair stood up in a fat rooster tail in back. He looked ridiculously happy.

Josh yanked the pole up about every five seconds to check his line. Drew squinted out at Mackerel Bay. The water winked in the late September sun. The ferry was just plowing into sight.

Drew Ellis loved being on the water. It helped him find a quiet place inside his head. At first his mind would let loose all the things he was worried about, and they'd run around between his ears—his dad's bad back; the sick puppy in his mom's shelter; his C-minus in math. But after a while, all that would fade. His head would give in to the rhythm, empty out the worries, rock with the water, and float.

Drew had thought maybe fishing would settle Josh down. But Josh Gordon was always about as settled as popcorn on a hot griddle.

"Look, Drew!" Josh said. "A crab!" He bent like a jackknife over the side. Drew pulled him back by his red jacket.

"Ahoy there! Mary Poppins!" a voice yelled. "How's the nanny business?"

"Jinx!" Josh squealed.

It was Jinx Harris, Drew's sixth-grade pal and cheerful torturer. Drew and Jinx weren't much alike. Drew was big. Jinx was small and wiry. Drew was quiet. Jinx could talk a mile a minute. Drew was slow to anger. Jinx had a hair trigger.

They would do anything for each other.

Jinx pulled the boat in by its anchor rope. He jumped aboard. "Well, if it isn't Crash Gordon." He endured a fierce hug from Josh. "Crash-landed on any good moose lately?"

"That was just a little mistake," Josh said.

4

"Look! We're fishing!" He pulled in his line with a jerk. Drew ducked the hook.

"And I got the best bait," Josh said. "It's a secret. Okay, I'll tell you. Peanut-butter cups!"

"Yeah. That's a well-kept secret all right." Jinx gave Drew a look.

Drew shrugged one shoulder. They were sitting in a rowboat in less than a foot of water, right beside the ferry dock. The only thing they could possibly catch was a cold.

Why ask some poor worm to give its life in vain?

Jinx settled himself in the back of the boat, on the stern seat. "I'm meeting Liz and Allie at your dad's diner," he told Drew. "I don't suppose you could come."

Drew ran a hand through his short, brown hair. They both knew Josh wasn't invited. The other kids had steered clear of him since two weeks before. They had made a life-size papier mâché moose for Maine Mania Day at school. Josh had tried to ride it—while it was still wet.

Moose mush.

Drew propped his back against the oarlock on the boat's side. "I can't today," he said. "But Josh's grandparents are coming up from Connecticut next Monday. I'll have the day off."

"They have a white horse with spots

that's named Pancake!" Josh yelled, loud as a ferry whistle.

"They really do," Drew told Jinx. "They own a horse farm."

"Yeah. And they have another one that's yellow. And she's named Maple Sugar. And I'm gonna..."

Josh stopped. He was staring up past the ferry landing, toward town.

"That's my daddy!"

The homemade pole clattered to the bottom of the boat. Josh scrambled up the side. He jumped off.

The boat tipped and righted itself. But by then, Drew had already landed on his backside in the water. The ocean is cold in September, his numb mind told him. Very cold.

Wide blue eyes and a smattering of freckles appeared above him. Jinx held out a hand. "Allow me, Miss Poppins."

But Drew was watching Josh streak along the beach. Josh was screeching, "Daddy! Daddy!"

"Josh, stop! Josh! Get back here!" Drew grabbed his backpack. He headed after the kid. "Josh! You have to stay with me!" Drew yelled.

He didn't say what the whole island knew. Josh had not seen his dad. He couldn't have.

Josh's father was in prison.

He was in prison because of Josh.

8

2
RETURN OF THE FEARSOME FOURSOME

Drew ran THUNK! into a solid wall of flesh by the ferry dock. "Sorry," he mumbled. The muscles belonged to Lonnie Bickford. THE OAF, Jinx called him. Drew was big. Lonnie was gigundo!

"Watch it, punk!" Lonnie spit. Lonnie was famous on the island. Or at least as famous as a high school kid could be. He'd been to juvenile hall in Portland, twice. He had two nose rings and a big hunk of metal that pierced his upper lip—the one he sneered with. Drew watched that lip. But Lonnie didn't say anything else. He just brushed past Drew and kept walking.

Josh was hanging over the ferry dock railing. He was staring toward town. "Here I am! Come back!" he shouted. Drew saw the flash of a blue shirt disappearing around the corner by Tinkhams' General Store. It could have been anybody.

He squeezed Josh's bony shoulder.

There was the rumble of an engine and the slosh of churned water, then the clatter of a ramp being lowered. The ferry was docking.

"Joshie! Hey! Look who's home early."

Darlene Gordon, Josh's mother, was coming down the boat ramp. She worked as a receptionist in a doctor's office on the mainland. Drew watched Josh after school until she got home.

Mrs. Gordon was thin and very, very pretty. She had blonde hair and thick eyelashes, like one of those models on the front of the magazines in the supermarket. She didn't look much like any mom Drew knew. But she kneeled right down on the rough wood of the dock and hugged Josh till he tried to wiggle free.

"Hey, handsome," she greeted Drew. She had a smile like a spotlight.

Drew felt his face get hot. "Hi, Mrs. Gordon."

He suddenly remembered he was sopping wet. Josh was soaked to the knees, too. Darlene Gordon must have noticed, but she didn't say anything.

"Come on, Josh," Mrs. Gordon said. Then she walked off, across Front Street, past the cluster of stores that formed Ragged Island's only town. Josh trailed behind. His cheek was smeared with red lipstick. He pulled out his plastic men again.

"Bye, Josh," Drew called. "See you tomorrow."

"That Josh is a menace," Jinx said from behind him.

"Yeah," said Drew. But something twanged in his stomach for the kid.

* * * *

"Mr. Gordon is in jail," Allie said. "But what does Josh have to do with it?" They were in a booth in Mel's Diner: Drew, Jinx, Allie, and Liz.

Allie was the only one who didn't know the story. All Drew could see of her was her shiny, straight black hair. She was bent over the table, making a little house out of toothpicks. Allie Davies was always making stuff. The whole world fit together in her head, sort of like those snap-together plastic building blocks.

"It was in the paper," Jinx said. "Tommy Gordon was dealing drugs. The cops got a tip. And when Sheriff Greenwood went to their house, Crash turned him in."

"Wrong." Liz shook her head. Her springy brown hair flew. Drew watched it. Then he caught himself watching it. Then he felt like a doofus. He felt that way a lot around Liz lately.

"Josh was playing with some toy," Liz said.

"A stuffed dog," said Drew. His voice cracked and he cleared his throat.

Liz nodded. "It was stuffed, all right. Josh pulled a baggie filled with white powder out of it—while the sheriff was standing right there. It was drugs."

"Surprise!" said Jinx. "Dumb kid."

"He was only four," Drew said.

"Oh," said Jinx. "Still, I bet his daddy was super mad at him!"

Sharon the waitress set a tray down on their table with a thump. Her pink lipstick and the pink barrettes in her hair matched her pink uniform. A hankie with pink roses peeked out of her pocket.

"SOMEONE," she said, "told me to bring

these sodas to the Fearsome Foursome. On the house."

Drew looked behind the counter. His dad was pouring a cup of coffee for Old Mr. Dawson. Jim Ellis winked. Mel's Diner used to be owned by somebody named Mel. Now Drew's father owned it and ran it—and practically lived in it.

Drew felt a little sting of guilt in his chest. His dad's diner was the real reason he was baby-sitting Josh. Mrs. Gordon paid him six dollars a day. But Drew didn't care about the money. He didn't even have anything he wanted to buy. The bills were stacked in a neat pile in the corner of his top dresser drawer.

He'd been afraid that his dad would ask him to help out at the diner. That was the thing. The diner was busy and loud. Drew didn't like craziness and confusion.

Drew's dad was the greatest—except

when the diner got too busy and waitresses didn't show up and dishwashers broke down and his back started to hurt. Then it was another story.

"Sharon, pick-up! Sharon!" his dad bellowed.

Drew didn't like confusion, and he didn't like being yelled at, either. He wondered what his friends would think if they knew he was being such a wimp.

"Why did everyone at Mel's diner laugh when they saw Drew's breakfast?" Jinx asked.

"Why?" Drew and Liz asked it together.

"They thought it was a big yolk!" Jinx giggled.

"Don't laugh," Allie warned the others. "He'll tell more of them!"

"So what are you guys going to find out about Ragged Island for the all-school project?" Liz asked.

"Dunno," Allie said. Her black head dipped closer to the tabletop.

"Now, do your research!" Jinx said in a breathy voice. He sounded just like Mrs. Lord, the oldest teacher at school. "Amazing facts! Fascinating secrets! That's what we're looking for!" He switched back into his own voice. "I saw you head for the library after school, Liz French. Forget it. Everybody already knows everything in all the books about this dinky place."

Liz elbowed him. Liz and Jinx were cousins. They always egged each other on. "So what do you suggest, Einstein?" Liz asked.

Jinx looked solemn. "I thought I'd try peeking in some windows," he said.

Just then Mrs. Firbush pushed through the door. Mrs. Firbush worked in the school cafeteria. She was short and square. She filled up the space by their booth perfectly.

"I know what you children did," she said.

They all froze.

"What's up, there, Margaret?" Old Mr. Dawson asked from his stool at the counter.

Mrs. Firbush was still staring at them. "Someone took my Rodney's clothes. Right

off the clothesline. His best shirt. And his boxer shorts, for goodness sake!"

Liz gave a little snort of a laugh. But she stifled it. Quick.

Mrs. Firbush stared at Jinx. Her bright red hair stuck up in clumps. "I know who made that scarecrow last fall and propped it on a commode on the school lawn."

"A commode?" Liz said. "You mean a toilet?"

Jinx's face looked innocent. Too innocent.

Then Mrs. Firbush was looking right at Drew. "And I know he wasn't strong enough to do it alone.

"That shirt was brand new. I want my husband's clothes back. And I'd better get them."

Allie spoke up. "Thank you for letting us know, Mrs. Firbush. We will have our eyes open for the thief. The REAL one." Allie had spunk. Somehow, she even managed to sound polite. Sitting there in the diner booth, in a "Question Authority" T-shirt, chin held high, she looked like royalty, like an angry princess. Her brown eyes looked straight at Mrs. Firbush and held for a moment. Then she turned to her friends.

"My log cabin's finished," Allie said. "How do you like it?" She pointed to a little house of toothpicks.

It was perfect.

3

The Legs in the Bushes

It was colder after school the next day. Drew zipped up his jacket. He heard a teacher yell, "Josh, slow down!" Then a flying object slammed into him. Josh's arms went around his waist.

"Hi, Drew!"

Oh, well. Another day, another black-and-blue mark. "Hi, Josh."

Josh had on the same pumpkin T-shirt as yesterday. He was holding a plastic bag stuffed with action figures.

"Where's your jacket?" Drew asked.

Josh shrugged. "Can we go to the secret hideout?" he asked.

"I guess. Sure," Drew said.

The secret hideout was really an old cottage. The owner was a summer visitor named Mrs. Cary. She set up an easel on the porch every summer and painted pictures of the island. The paintings were terrible, but she was nice. She didn't mind if kids played on her property.

The cottage sat way back from Maine Street, in a pocket of trees. They had to push through a gate and up a long, bushy path.

Drew held back a branch. Josh wasn't beside him. He turned around. "Hey, Josh, get down from that tree."

"I'm scouting," Josh said.

"Scouting for what?"

"Intergalactic space spies! My daddy's

22

going to take me up on the space station someday. You can spit down on the moon from up there."

Josh crashed down from the tree into a heap at Drew's feet. He grabbed Drew's jeans to help himself up and almost pulled Drew over instead.

Drew had always wondered what it was like to be a big brother. If this was it, he figured he owed his own big brother Rob a giant apology.

They walked around to the rear of the cottage and lay on their stomachs on the back porch. The boards were warm from the sun. Drew could smell pine trees, mixed with the salt of the ocean—a Ragged Island smell.

Josh dumped out all his toys.

"These are your guys, and these are my guys." He picked up a soldier. "Now I say,

'Get off the Earth, you monsters! Or we will destroy you!'"

Drew raised the arm of a plastic monster with one hideous eye and green skin. He lowered his voice. "Stay your hand, Earthling. We come in peace."

"No, no," Josh said. "Now you say you're going to eat us all up!"

Drew moved up another figure. This one had fangs and webbed feet. He made his voice high. "We will live in the oceans. You may keep the land. We will work together for

24

the good of all."

"No, no!" Josh pushed at Drew's arm. "That's not how you play! You have to try to destroy me! Come on! Now you say, 'I'll smash you all with my laser cannon!' Go ahead!"

"Why?" Drew said.

"Because! That's how you do it!" Josh sat back on his heels and took a deep breath. Drew could see him gathering what little six-year-old patience he had. "See, I'm the good guy and you're the bad guy. The bad guy tries to kill everybody and I save the Earth. That's how you play it. Come on. I'll tell you what to say."

"Thanks a bunch," Drew thought.

Josh set a figure on each knee. He held one up. "See, this is The Raider. He's a Good-Heart. That's all the good guys, what I call them. And all the guys that look like this"—

he held up the monster—"they're bad. They stink and they do bad stuff." He banged the bad guy against his knee and leaned low over it. "You're the Evil Mean Bad Guy," he told it. "You are…"

A crash. It came from the front of the cottage.

"What's that?" Josh said.

"Is somebody there?" Drew called.

Silence.

Then Drew heard a scrape, like a chair on wood. It sounded like it came from the front porch, on the far side of the building. The black Lab next door started barking its head off. They were deep, rasping barks.

"Evil Mean Bad Guy." The thought echoed in Drew's head. He shook it away.

"Hello? Who's there?" Drew shouted.

The dog was still barking. Drew argued silently with himself:

"Somebody's there. Out front."

"It's probably just another dog."

"This doesn't feel right."

"It's okay. This is the island. We're fine."

"But we're here all alone."

"Drew?" Josh asked.

Drew shook his head and put his finger to his lips. He swept the toys back into their bag. Then he bent down and whispered, "Climb on my back. We have to escape them."

Josh climbed up. "Who?"

"The space spies, of course," Drew answered. "They must have heard us."

"Intergalactic space spies," Josh said. He giggled and got a strangle grip around Drew's neck.

They could cut through the woods behind the cottage, to Drew's house. But it was probably safer to head toward people. And the closest people were back on Maine Street. To get there, they'd have to go past the front of the cottage, right by the noise.

Drew took a deep breath. He headed around the side of the building, toward the path.

A stack of wooden shutters was overturned on the front porch. Drew walked more quickly. The dog was still barking. He was barking at them now, Drew thought. He pushed through the bushes. The path had never seemed so long.

They were halfway to the gate. He'd been foolish to panic. It must have been a dog. Drew slowed down.

Then he saw him. The bottom half of him, anyway. Where the bushes were thin, near the ground, Drew could see blue jeans, brown, scuffed shoes, and bare ankles. He noticed the bare ankles. Then the legs were coming closer through the bushes.

"Hold on tight!" Drew told Josh.

He started to run.

There would be someone on Maine Street. There had to be.

"What if there isn't?" he asked himself.

Drew could hear branches snapping behind him.

29

EVIL MEAN BAD GUY. The hairs stood up on the back of his neck.

More snapping.

Hurry!

A few more feet. A few more steps.

Drew crashed through the gate. He ran down Maine Street, past two houses, before he turned back to look.

No one was coming.

No one had followed them through the gate. Maine Street was just—Maine Street. Drew watched as a woman with a long braid settled her baby in a car seat. A man on a bike pedaled by. Mr. Firbush—the one with the lost underwear—walked out of the Millers' driveway. Everything was normal.

Drew was sweaty and panting. He didn't know whether to feel relieved, or just stupid. Had that guy been after them? It seemed so unreal. But he could still feel the panic pumping through his chest.

That was when it hit him for the first time. He wasn't just hanging out after school with a first grader. He was responsible for Josh. If anything happened to the little runt it would be Drew's fault.

The very same runt, meanwhile, bounced up and down on Drew's back.

"That was fun!" he said. "Let's do it again!"

＊ ＊ ＊ ＊

Drew swiveled back and forth on a stool at the diner's counter. He stared at his math book. He'd had his supper: chowder and salad his dad gave him and mashed potatoes and apple pie from Sharon. Drew always ate at the diner when his mom stayed over on the mainland. Barbara Ellis was a veterinarian. Monday was her regular turn at the night clinic in Bellport.

Drew didn't know if he should tell his dad about the man in the bushes. When it happened, it had seemed real. It was scary. But now Drew thought maybe he had freaked for no reason. And he was a little afraid to tell his dad. What if he made Drew bring Josh straight to the diner after school every day? That would be a disaster. So Drew didn't say anything. Whoever it had been, everything was all right now.

"...wrong!" A hand slapped the counter. Old Mr. Dawson and Joe Crocksford were down at the end. Other people watched TV for entertainment. Mr. Dawson and Joe Crocksford argued.

Old Mr. Dawson chortled. "Nope. I'm tellin' ya. Bald as a cue ball," he said.

"Margaret Firbush?" Joe Crocksford shook his head. "You're full of it, old man."

"It's a wig. Bet you a jelly-filled," said Mr. Dawson.

"I'll just take that bet," Mr. Crocksford replied.

Mr. Dawson took out his bottom set of teeth and set them on a saucer. He sighed in relief.

"Any more news about that Gordon boy?" he asked.

Did he mean Josh? Drew forgot about math.

"Cryin' shame." Old Mr. Dawson shook his head. "Nice boy like that."

"Nice, my foot," said Joe Crocksford. "Tell that to the kids he got hooked on drugs. Tommy Gordon was a druggie, Everett."

Oh. Not Josh. They were talking about Josh's father.

"Should have known Darlene Sheehy would end up with a man like that," Joe

Crocksford went on. "That girl always did have a wild streak about a mile wide."

Mr. Dawson slurped his coffee. "Tommy Gordon fixed my outboard for me. Remember? That time I got stuck out on the clam flats?"

"Well, that doesn't exactly make him a saint," Mr. Crocksford said. He moved his toothpick to the other corner of his mouth.

"Helped Mike Cappella, too," Mr. Dawson said. "Mike was real friendly with that Gordon character.

"Steady boy, that Mike Cappella. Good lobster fisherman. Remember when he first started fixing up that boat of his?"

"I think he was only about sixteen," said Mr. Crocksford.

"Fifteen," said Mr. Dawson. "*Island Pony*, he called her. Crazy kid. Who ever would've thought he would still be fishing in her?"

"Well, now, talk about BALD!" Mr. Crocksford said. "I bet Mikey hasn't had a strand of hair left since he was twenty-two. His papa was the same way."

"Miracle of nature," said Mr. Dawson. Both men laughed. They headed for the door.

Drew looked at their empty places. He jumped off his stool. "Excuse me? Mr. Dawson?" Both men turned around.

Drew pointed to the counter. "I think you forgot—" The teeth still sat there on the plate.

"HA!" said Mr. Crocksford. "Forgot 'em again! You owe me a bear claw, old man!"

"Dang!"

"Mr. Dawson?" Drew asked. "Did something happen? About Josh Gordon's father?"

"Well," said Mr. Dawson. "I thought everybody knew." He pushed his teeth past

35

his lips. They clicked as they slid into place. "That Tommy Gordon escaped from jail. Just walked away from the prison library in Thomaston two days ago."

4

THE BOY WHO CRIED WOLF

Sheriff Greenwood's car was sitting at the curb when Drew and Josh left school the next afternoon. As they got close, the window slid down. Something slid in Drew's stomach, too.

"Hey, there, Josh." The sheriff's voice was kind. "Want a ride in the cruiser?"

Josh's squeal hurt Drew's ears. The little kid clambered into the front seat without a backward glance.

"Come on, Drew," the sheriff said. "I'll give you a lift."

Drew climbed into the back. A metal grid divided the car in half. He wondered if people who saw him would think he had committed a crime. Maybe he had. Was it a crime to report seeing an escaped convict if you weren't really sure?

That's what Drew had done. First he'd told his dad about the guy in the bushes and about Tommy Gordon. Jim Ellis threw down his newspaper. He gave the hassock a good kick. "Drew Ellis, how many times do I have to—"

"I know, Dad!" Drew said. "I should have told you right away. But..."

"But what?"

Drew just stared at the paper strewn on the floor.

His dad groaned and rubbed the back of

his neck. "But you thought maybe I'd go four-star-general on you, right? Maybe I'd order you to report immediately after school and stay where I could see you every minute? 'Oh—and by the way, my sneakers need spit-shining, soldier'?"

Drew winced. "Something like that, yeah."

His father shook his head. "Well, I might have, at that." He took a deep breath. Then he gave Drew's shoulder a shake. "Come to me right away next time, hear me? Don't you ever wait till you get in over your head to ask for help." He frowned. "Remind me later that I'm really mad at you," he said. "But what do you want to do now?"

They decided Drew would call Darlene Gordon first.

Darlene told Drew she hadn't seen her ex-husband. "But then, I wouldn't," she said.

"He wouldn't come around here." For a minute, she was silent. "Drew Ellis," she said then, "don't you let that man near my kid. Do you hear me?"

Drew heard her. But what did she think he could do? Next he and his dad called the police station. Before they knew it, the sheriff was sitting on their sofa with a picture of Tommy Gordon. He called it a "mug shot." Drew couldn't believe what was happening.

All that was last night. Now the police car drove slowly down Maine Street and around the curve to Spruce Road. It slid past the Ellis driveway and onto the dirt turnabout in front of Josh's house.

Josh was bouncing with excitement. "Can I turn on the...?" The rest was drowned out by the scream of the siren. A blue light flared against the small ranch house in front of them. Then Josh's hand was swallowed up in the sheriff's big one and the siren stopped.

"Go get yourself some cookies or something, huh?" Sheriff Greenwood was telling Josh. "I need to talk to Drew here." He handed Josh a key. "You know how to use this?"

"Sure." Josh took off across the grass. The key surprised Drew. Mrs. Gordon didn't usually lock her house. Most islanders didn't.

"Mrs. Gordon asked me to give you the key," Sheriff Greenwood said.

"Did you find Tommy Gordon?" Drew asked.

The sheriff shook his head. "We had four cruisers over from the mainland last night. Went door to door. Covered the whole island from tip to tip."

41

"Then where can he be hiding?"

The sheriff turned around in his seat. "Far from here, that's where. Look, you seem like a smart kid. We've watched all the ferries since the escape. Nothing. It's like I told you and your dad last night. Ragged Island is the last place this guy would go. It's too small. He'd be caught for sure."

Drew shook his head. "But Josh saw him too. He'd know his own father."

The sheriff gave a bark of laughter. "That one? He barely knows which planet he's on." He pulled out a clipboard and wrote something on it. "There's nothing here for Tommy Gordon. Mrs. Gordon divorced him months ago. Believe me. He's long gone."

He got out of the car and opened Drew's door. Drew realized then that there were no handles on the inside.

"Look, kid, you let your imagination get the best of you. It happens." The sheriff sighed. "Every time a guy escapes from jail, we get sightings all over the place. If the police followed up on every call, every person who saw someone acting sneaky or overheard some plot, we'd never have time to do our real jobs. Sure, people get nervous. Can't say I really blame them. But we've spent a lot of time and manpower on this already, all for nothing. Tommy Gordon is nowhere near Ragged Island."

Sheriff Greenwood folded his big body back into the car. He rolled down the window. "You're a good kid," he said. "You focus your attention on Josh. He's plenty of trouble all by himself. Mrs. Gordon trusts you. Just don't let your imagination run wild, okay?"

Drew felt a flush of heat move up his

neck. "Okay," he said.

His dad had said it too: "I trust you to know what you can handle, Drew."

Maybe adults should trust him a little less, Drew thought. He didn't know what the heck to think anymore.

Part of him really wanted to quit this baby-sitting job. Josh was a pest, the little goof. But what if Tommy Gordon really was out there? Drew was the only one who thought it was possible. Yeah, the guy was Josh's dad. But he was also a criminal. A new baby-sitter wouldn't know to be on the lookout.

When Drew went inside the house, he found Josh was building a fort out of all the sofa and chair cushions.

"I ran the siren!" he screeched.

"I noticed." Drew turned down the sound on the Florida theme park commercial that was blaring from the TV.

Josh got still. He stared at the screen. "My daddy's going to take me there someday," he said. "Roller coasters and stuff. He promised."

Drew winced. The kid didn't have a clue. "How about a snack?"

"Yes! I want a peanut butter and potato chip sandwich! With pickles!" There was no bread. Drew made a sandwich on a hot-dog roll. No milk, either. Drew mixed up some juice. He settled Josh in front of the TV.

Then he settled himself at the dining room table. He pushed some papers, a pile of mail, and a notebook aside to make space for his English homework.

BRRRRRING!!!

Drew jumped a foot. Then he got up and grabbed for the phone on the kitchen counter. "Hello?"

Someone took a breath. There was a moment of silence. Then a click.

"Wrong number," Drew thought.

But he felt strange about it. What if it was Tommy Gordon?

"Wrong number," he told himself again. Maybe he was getting paranoid. He sat back down and turned a page. Then he turned it back. It was awfully hard to care about compound sentences right now.

BRRRRRing!!!

Oh, boy. He let the phone ring twice more, then picked it up. "Hello?"

"Drew? It's Liz!"

Drew could practically see her brown hair flying.

"Drew?"

"Yeah."

"I'm at the diner. Everybody's talking about last night. All the police and stuff."

Drew wasn't surprised that people knew his connection to the police hunt already. News spread like wildfire on Ragged Island. Pretty soon everybody would know he was the dumb kid who panicked and called the police for nothing.

"Drew?" Liz's voice said, "Meet us at Cabin 4 after supper, okay?" Cabin 4 was part of Rocky Point Bed and Breakfast. Rocky Point sat near the north end of the island. Liz's mom ran it. The cabin was the friends' unofficial meeting place.

"I don't know, Liz. I don't really..."

"Hey!" Liz said. "Cabin 4 after supper." The line clicked off.

Drew sighed. He flopped down beside Josh and stared at the TV screen. Josh was riveted. His hair still stuck up in back, just like the roadrunner's tail in the cartoon.

Drew didn't think he was ready to talk to

the other kids yet. He needed some time to think. It wasn't like him to be scared. But he was. Now he was supposed to forget about it. But he couldn't. The adults all acted as though everything was settled. But it wasn't settled for Drew. There was just something WRONG about it all.

BRRRRRING!!!

Not again.

"I'll get it!" Josh scrambled up. Drew pulled in his legs, but not quickly enough. He rubbed his shin. Outside, a door slammed. Through the window Drew saw a brown pickup pulling away. Mrs. Gordon was teetering across the grass on high heels, her arms filled with groceries. He went to help.

"You didn't tell Josh anything about...anything?" Mrs. Gordon whispered.

Drew shook his head, and Darlene Gordon smiled.

"Then that's fine," she said. She turned on the radio. Music blared over the sound of the TV.

"Everything's fine. Fine, fine, fine!" Mrs. Gordon threw her arms wide. She turned around and around, laughing.

Josh ran in from the kitchen. He started twirling too. They got dizzy and collided and laughed harder. Then a heel on Mrs. Gordon's shoe broke. She bumped up against the grocery bag on the dining room table. Everything went sliding to the floor— groceries, papers, and Drew's homework.

Darlene Gordon stopped. Her smile faded. Her eyes filled with tears.

"I'll get it," said Drew. "No problem." He was down on his knees scooping up paper towels and butter and pushing books and papers back into his backpack as fast as he could.

"Just take Josh outside for a minute. Okay?" Tears were running down Mrs. Gordon's cheeks.

Drew sat on the back steps. Josh was riding a stick horse all around the yard.

Drew watched for a while. Then he remembered the phone. "Josh, was that phone call for your mom?" he asked.

Josh trotted over. He put his forehead against Drew's. "NO!"

He trotted in a circle again. "That was my daddy. And guess what? He's going to take me for a ride on a pony. Real soon! He promised."

Josh made his stick horse rear up. "It's a secret," he added.

"Oh." Drew said.

Oh, no.

5

THE FACE IN THE WINDOW

"It's simple," Jinx said. "We just have to find Tommy Gordon."

"Right." Liz surprised Drew by agreeing.

Drew stared out the window at the shadowy pines in the dusk behind Cabin 4. It had been a relief to tell Jinx and Liz about the guy in the bushes, about the phone calls, and about the way Darlene Gordon laughed and cried and acted kind of strange. For once, Jinx hadn't even teased him. But now his friends were galloping ahead, sort of like

Joshie on his stick horse.

"The police say there isn't any Tommy Gordon to find," Drew said. "Maybe they're right. Maybe I just panicked."

"No way," Liz said. "We know you."

"Your problem is, you're used to adults believing you," Jinx told him. "Get over it."

"You and Josh both saw somebody, right?" said Liz. "So if it wasn't Tommy Gordon, who was it?"

Drew felt his eyes sting. His friends were the best. "But they're the police," he said. "They know their stuff."

"They couldn't search everywhere," Liz said. "Maybe we know places they wouldn't think of. Besides, even if Josh's dad isn't on the island, what harm can it do to look?"

"I wonder if there's a reward for finding him!" Jinx said. He flopped onto one of the twin beds. "We could be rich!"

"But why would he come back here?" Drew frowned. "That's what I can't figure out."

"The criminal always returns to the scene of the crime," Jinx offered. They looked at him. He shrugged. "Okay. That's lame."

"Maybe he left some drugs on the island?" Liz asked. "Or he came back for a stash of money, maybe."

"Maybe he wants to get back at Crash," Jinx said. "For getting him arrested."

They all stared at each other.

"He does keep showing up around Josh," Drew said slowly.

"That's crazy!" Liz declared. "Josh is just a little kid. Yes, he helped get his dad arrested. But he didn't know any better."

"Yeah," said Jinx. "But who knows what happens to guys in jail? I mean, they're all crazy in there, right? They spend weeks sharpening spoons to make them into weapons. They strangle each other for fun. Escaped convicts are the guys they make all those scary movies about. Maybe Tommy Gordon's nuts. Maybe he's been sitting there for two whole years, just thinking about how it's all that little kid's fault."

Jinx got a funny look on his face. He stared at Drew. "Jeesh," he said. "And when the paper comes out, it's gonna say someone called the police. It's gonna say that person saw Tommy Gordon. Tommy's going to know it was you."

Drew watched Liz shiver. "We've got to find Tommy Gordon," she said.

The door to Cabin 4 banged against the wall. Allie blew in, straight black hair flying. "Sorry I'm late," she said. "It was my turn for dishes." Allie had a bunch of little sisters and brothers. Washing dishes at her house could take about a week. She still had an apron wrapped twice around her waist. It read, Cleanliness Is Next to Impossible.

"Here," she said. She passed a piece of paper to each of them.

Drew looked at his. "You, too?" he asked. Allie looked at him calmly. "We have to find Tommy Gordon," she said.

On Allie's paper was a list of things an escaped convict would need. Jinx looked up from it. "You're slipping," he told Allie. "It's not in alphabetical order."

Drew read the list aloud: "Food. Clothes. Money. A place to sleep. A boat?"

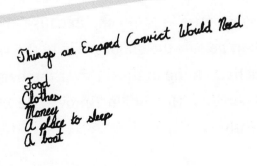

Things an Escaped Convict Would Need

Food
Clothes
Money
A place to sleep
A boat

"For getting on and off the island," Allie said. "Makes sense, if he didn't come on the ferry."

"Clothes," Drew said again.

"Yeah. He would need to get rid of that orange thingy they all wear," Allie said.

"Wait," Drew said. "He did it. HE did it. He took those clothes!"

"Huh?" Jinx said.

"Mrs. Firbush's clothes!" Drew told him. "Maybe Tommy Gordon really is here. Maybe HE took them."

"Right!" Allie said. "Brilliant connection. Here, have a peanut butter cookie."

Drew put his hand out for one. But he lost his appetite mid-reach. Because that was when he saw the ghoul's face in the window. His hand hung in the air over the baggie full of cookies. He couldn't move. He couldn't breathe.

It had big, googly eyes.

"Why me?" was his first thought. Why didn't one of the other kids see it?

Then Liz did. She took one step closer to the window. Drew could see Liz's reflection staring next to the other face. The reflection opened its mouth.

"AIEEEEEE!" Liz screamed.

"EEEEEEYA!" There was an answering scream from outside. Then a crash. The face disappeared.

Jinx was quickest. He ran around back.

They heard him yell, "Owen McBride, you little twerp!" Then he was dragging the ghoul into the cabin by the hood of its sweatshirt.

Owen was a third grader, a friend of Allie's brother Daniel. As a ghoul, he was strictly a lightweight. When he wasn't peeking into dark windows, he was just a little kid in thick glasses.

Owen blinked. He looked like an owl.

"You scared the spit out of me, Owen McBride!" Liz was mad. "Where do you get off, spying on us?"

Owen blinked again. "Sorry. I didn't mean to frighten you," he said. "The woodpile slipped."

"Yeah, right." Jinx gave Owen's sweatshirt a shake. "But what were you doing up on the woodpile in the first place?"

"The school project, of course," Owen said.

"The project," Allie repeated.

"Yes!" Owen looked around at all the faces staring at him. "You know. Fascinating facts about Ragged Island. I was over at Daniel's and I heard Allie talking on the phone about Josh Gordon's father. It sounded promising!"

"Promising?" Allie repeated.

"Yes! Where is Tommy Gordon? We could discover the island's biggest secret of all!"

"We?" Allie repeated.

"Toss him out of here," Liz said.

"You can't do that!" Owen cried.

Jinx began hauling Owen toward the door.

Owen grabbed onto the door frame.

"No! You can't!"

"Watch me," Jinx said.

"You can't..."

Jinx picked him up. He stepped over the

sill. Owen held on to the frame. His body flew straight out, like a flag.

"You can't...because I know something... you don't!" Owen choked out.

"Set him down," said Drew.

"And this had better be good!" Liz added.

Owen stood across the room, as far from Jinx as he could get. "I ran to Tinkhams' store for my ma today before school. We needed more...um...toilet paper." Owen's face got red.

"Great," Drew thought. "Spying is okay, but TP embarrasses him."

"Anyhow, Mrs. Tinkham was really mad," Owen continued. "Somebody stole a whole crate of eggs from the store. That couldn't be a coincidence, could it?" He looked at Drew. "Don't you see? It's on the list. I heard you through the window. Food is on the list! Tommy Gordon needed food!"

"He's right," Allie declared.

Liz still wanted to throw Owen out, but the others thought he might as well help. So Owen McBride was sworn to secrecy, and they began to organize their own hunt for Tommy Gordon.

Jinx and Allie were put in charge of searching for sleeping places. They'd also look for any unfamiliar boats tied up in the smaller coves. They would need pictures if they found anything, and Allie was a great shot with a camera. Drew insisted they always search in teams, so no one would have to face Tommy Gordon alone. "And if we find anything, we tell my dad right away, okay?" Drew asked.

Everybody nodded.

Owen would be a back-up searcher. Liz offered to talk to Mrs. Tinkham and the other store owners to find out if anyone had seen the egg thief. Drew agreed he should interview Darlene Gordon. The more they knew about Tommy Gordon, the better chance they had of finding him.

The other kids also decided to take turns hanging out with Drew and Josh after school. It seemed the most likely place for Tommy Gordon to show up, and there was safety in numbers.

"I'll use my baby-sitting money to get each of us one of those disposable cameras," Drew said. "We'll need proof if we find him."

"What does he look like, anyhow?" Liz asked.

"Big," Jinx said. "Hairy. Like an escaped convict."

"He has black hair," Drew said. "And a tattoo of a teardrop right in the corner of one eye."

"Yuck!" said Liz.

"It's small, but you can see it," Drew said. "Sheriff Greenwood showed my dad and me a picture." Drew looked at his watch. "It's 7:40. I have to get home."

"Sorry, Drew," Allie said. "But it's 8:07." She held out her arm and tapped her watch. "This one's always right."

"Uh-oh," said Drew. "I told my mom I'd be home by 8. I've got to go. Can everybody report back tomorrow night?"

They all nodded.

So it was settled.

As he biked back home up Front Street, past Tinkhams' store and the ferry wharf, Drew was almost convinced they would do it. They would really find an escaped convict and turn him in.

Of course, that was BEFORE Lonnie Bickford and a couple of his less-than-tasteful friends jumped off the sidewalk and ran at Drew's bike, waving their arms and yelling and hooting.

"I'm the bogeyman!"

"BLBLBLBLEH!"

"Watch out, Ellis! I'm gonna get ya!"

Then they laughed like maniacs.

Okay. Word was out all over the island that he'd called the police. So now it was official. Everyone knew he was scared of Tommy Gordon. Drew pedaled on. At least now, whatever happened, his friends were going to help. Things were bound to get better.

But that night he dreamed he was being chased by an Evil Mean Bad Guy. It had two long fangs, and big wet tears kept squeezing out of its eyes and falling at its webbed feet.

6
DEAD ENDS

Finding a desperate criminal was not as easy as it sounded.

The egg robbery was the first dead end. Liz found out that the eggs had been stolen from the back of Tinkhams' store early in the morning, before Mrs. Tinkham opened. Nothing else was missing. Nobody had seen a thing. Maybe Tommy Gordon stole the eggs. Maybe he didn't.

Jinx and Allie checked out the Cary cottage. It was locked up tight. They found two boats in Quahog Bay that they couldn't identify. But Mr. Crocksford recognized them. They both belonged to visitors.

Owen got a map of the island and made a copy at the library. They started crossing out each place they had checked with a red X.

That left talking to Darlene Gordon.

She was already home when Josh and Drew got there on Thursday, two hours after school let out. She was watching TV and eating handfuls of popcorn.

"Mommy! It's us!" Josh announced in his loudest voice. "Drew Good-Heart and Joshua Gordon Good-Heart!"

"Ah, come closer, then," Mrs. Gordon said. She jumped up and spread her hands out like claws. "Because Mommy needs her supper!" She made a scary face and started stalking Josh. She walked with her legs all stiff, and she growled a lot.

Josh loved it. He giggled and squealed and ran around the sofa. Then he made a dash for safety under the dining room table. But the monster mom grabbed him. She swung him around. Then she hugged him tight.

"Mine! All mine!" she growled. She nuzzled his cheek until Josh wiggled and shrieked. "Tell me you love me!" she ordered him. "Tell me you love me, or I'll

71

squeeze you till you squeak!" Josh buried his face in her neck. "I love you, Mommy," he said.

Darlene laughed and gave him a big, smacking kiss. "You're going to be a heartbreaker. You know that?" She tumbled down onto the couch. They were both out of breath. Then Darlene noticed Drew still standing there.

"Hey, sit down, handsome," she said. "I need to talk to you tonight." She reached for the remote and flipped the channel on the TV.

Drew looked for a place to sit. Empty cans and paper plates sat on every surface. The recliner held a rolled-up rug. A bent, greasy pizza box perched on the seat of the rocking chair.

Mrs. Gordon grinned at him. "The maid and the butler both quit this morning. What can I say?" She tossed the pizza box under the coffee table.

Drew sat. He looked at the TV. Little scrub brushes with eyes were scouring a kitchen sink.

A hunk of blue canvas appeared in front of his nose.

"Look what I got, Drew!" Josh pushed up against Drew's knees. "It's a backpack, and it's just exactly like yours!"

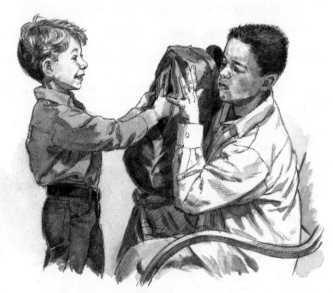

"Uh-huh. Nice," Drew said. He started to nod, but his nose hit the pack.

"And I'm gonna fill it up with books and stuff. Then I'll be just like you." Josh put the straps over his shoulder. They fell right back off. The pack was too big for him. "Do you have any more books I can put in it?" he asked.

"Josh," Mrs. Gordon said. "Bath time."

Josh made a stubborn face. He didn't look up or move from the sofa.

"Bubbles, bubbles, bubbles," his mom said in a sing-song voice. Then both Josh's dimples appeared. "They're in that big bottle in the hall closet," his mother told him.

He ran down the hall toward the bathroom.

Drew waited until he heard water running. But before he could ask about

Tommy Gordon, Mrs. Gordon was talking.

"You're a good kid, Drew," she said. "I trust you. But something's missing from my house, and I need to know. Did you take it?"

"Huh?"

"It's okay. Maybe you wanted to use it, but I need it back." She was sitting on the edge of the sofa, leaning toward him. "This is important."

"I didn't take anything," Drew said. He couldn't think. What was she talking about?

"Well, did you have any other kids in here? Some friends, maybe?"

"No," said Drew. He wanted to say more. He wanted to tell her he would never steal. He wanted to tell her he was trying to help her annoying son, and that this wasn't fair. But nothing came out. The flat voice of a local newscaster buzzed from the TV.

"Hey, this is no game!" Mrs. Gordon had

grabbed Drew's arm. "The door was locked. You were the only one in here!"

"Maybe Tommy Gordon knows where you keep the key," Drew thought. "Maybe he's been in here." But he didn't say it.

Mrs. Gordon took a deep breath. She shoved her blonde hair behind her ears and sat back. "Okay," she said. "I've been there. I know it's hard to admit it when you do something wrong. So if you have it, you can just leave it back here in the house, all right?" She flashed a smile. Her lipstick was bright, like red plastic. "No harm done."

Drew didn't say anything. He didn't move. In the quiet, the newscaster's voice suddenly seemed loud.

"Police reported a possible sighting today of a man who escaped from the Thomaston prison Sunday morning. Local authorities in Sandstone, Connecticut, say that a man resembling Thomas Gordon was seen in a public park this morning. Police have been searching for Gordon since he slipped past prison guards on Sunday. Sources say Gordon has family members in the Sandstone area."

That was that, then. The adults had been right. Tommy Gordon wasn't even on the island.

That was that.

7

MISSING MOM

The next day, Drew sat on a stone wall in the schoolyard watching Crash Gordon's latest victim. Liz was lying flat in the grass. She gave a blood-chilling howl. Then she rolled her eyes up and thrashed around. She made a much better bad guy than Drew did.

Drew sighed. It was time to give up all the good guy–bad guy stuff in his own head. Big, brave Drew. He was going to find the nasty, bad convict and save the little kid.

Ha! Some hero he was. He had let a six-year-old dump him into Mackerel Bay. He'd run away just because a guy was standing behind some bushes. He'd let himself get freaked by a telephone hang-up. He'd embarrassed himself in front of his friends AND the local policeman. And now he'd been accused of stealing a...something. He didn't even know what!

It had not been a good week.

Liz sat down next to him. Their shoulders touched. Drew tried not to notice.

"They did say a POSSIBLE sighting," Liz said. Drew had told her everything at lunch. "It's not for sure that Tommy Gordon is in Connecticut."

Drew stared at Josh. "What's he doing now?" he asked.

Josh walked smack into the tire swing. He turned around in circles. Then he flopped on the grass. One foot stuck straight up. It twitched.

"He's practicing dying," Liz said.

"Oh."

"I really think you saw him, Drew."

Drew kicked at his backpack. "You don't have to stay, you know. I don't think we need guarding anymore."

"Yeah. That's okay." Liz pawed through her fanny pack. "I want to talk to Mrs. Firbush when she leaves anyhow."

"Mrs. Firbush? I thought all those cafeteria people went home early."

"She had to do inventory or something," Liz said. "You know, counting ketchup bottles."

"I almost forgot about those clothes she thinks Jinx and I took." Drew's eyes narrowed. "Why talk to her?"

Liz dumped the contents of her fanny pack out on the wall. She moved her disposable camera aside. "I had an idea about the project—you know, Ragged Island secrets. Gramp says she's worked at the school forever. Wouldn't it be cool to find out about the wildest pranks kids ever played here? I thought she might remember some."

"She'll remember some, all right," Drew said. "But will she tell you? She'll probably bite your little head off instead."

"No. Mrs. Firbush likes me," Liz declared.

"She does?"

"Yup," Liz said.

"How come?"

Liz grinned. "Maybe it's my intelligence or my great sense of humor and natural all-around cuteness?"

Drew just stopped himself from agreeing with her. He watched Josh lurch upside down over the tire swing and pretend to die.

"Maybe it's because you're so humble," he said.

Liz shrugged. "Maybe. Hey, Drew, do you have an extra pen?" she asked. "I can't find mine."

"I think so." He unzipped his backpack and fished around in the bottom. His fingers touched something he couldn't identify.

He pulled out a small, battered notebook. "Hey, this isn't mine." Drew looked down at the other navy backpack by his feet. "Oh," he said. "This is Josh's pack." He started to shove the notebook back in the pack. Then he stopped. He looked at it more carefully

Initials on the inside cover said DSG. It took only a second to figure out who that was. DSG. Darlene Sheehy Gordon. Drew flipped through the pages. It looked like accounts or something. Lots of initials and numbers. Maybe it was something from the

doctor's office where Mrs. Gordon worked. Drew snapped it shut. He put it back in Josh's pack. There were three or four other books in there.

"That pack must weigh a ton!" he thought.

But what was Josh doing with his mother's notebook?

Drew felt a poke on his arm.

"Drew? A pen?" Liz said.

"Oh, yeah. Sorry." Drew dug a pen out of his own backpack and forgot all about Liz. He was almost sure that notebook was the thing that was missing from Darlene Gordon's house. Josh had taken it.

Drew would have to tell Mrs. Gordon where the notebook was. But would she believe he hadn't taken it?

* * *

As it turned out, Drew didn't have a

chance to find out. He forgot all about the notebook. He had bigger worries. Darlene Gordon didn't come home that day.

Drew waited at Josh's house until both the 4:20 and the 5:35 ferries had come and gone. Then he left a note on the door and hustled Josh down to the diner. It was definitely time for Drew to talk to his dad.

What would happen when Josh found out the latest? Not only was his daddy a jailbird, but now his mother was gone, too.

8

LET'S MAKE A DEAL

"She's gone?" Jinx said. "Wow. This is getting good!" Drew had dropped Josh off with his dad at the diner. When he left, the kid was happily squeezing ketchup onto a plate in the shape of a Blob from the planet Ergon.

Now Drew and Jinx were walking along Pocket Beach to North Point, looking for strange boats. "Do you think maybe Darlene's helping Tommy?" Jinx asked.

Drew stared at the sandpipers zipping

along in the foam at the water's edge. With their long legs and jerky movements, the birds looked like wind-up toys.

"I don't think so. How could she? He's supposed to be in Connecticut."

"Come off it," Jinx said. Drew just stared at the tide line, and Jinx grabbed his shoulder. He gave him a shake. "Hey. Stop feeling sorry for yourself and stop worrying about that little kid. You're gonna give yourself zits. Drew!"

"Huh? Oh, sorry." Drew blinked at him. "What?"

Jinx shook his head. "I've got a bulletin for you, Miss Poppins," he said. "Come on." He led the way up a sand dune. They sat down in a hollow, out of the wind.

"Drew, I know Tommy Gordon is on Ragged Island. And I can prove it," Jinx declared. "Wait till you hear what I found out this afternoon."

Suddenly Drew realized Jinx was bursting with news. "I thought you went to the dentist this afternoon."

"I did. And guess who goes to the same dentist and who also had an appointment. We took the same ferry to Bellport."

"Who?"

"The OAF!"

"Lonnie Bickford?"

"Well, it wasn't Little Miss Muffet!"

Drew thought about Miss Muffet sporting two nose rings and leather jacket, jumping out at him and howling as he rode by on his bike. He shook his head.

"What's Lonnie Bickford got to do with anything?" he asked.

"That's what I'm trying to tell you," Jinx said. "First of all, he's the one who stole those eggs from behind Tinkhams'. He and his little friend—that skinny guy, about eight feet tall, with the missing front tooth? They were laughing about it. They plastered some high school teacher's house with eggs."

"Oh."

"Yeah. Very classy."

"So Tommy Gordon didn't take those eggs." Drew leaned back on his elbow in the sand.

"No. But you haven't heard the good part." Jinx leaned toward him. "Just as we hit the harbor, The OAF pulls this wad of money out of his pocket. He tells Stretch, there, that he's going to meet Tommy Gordon." Jinx put on his mimic face and a gruff voice. "He says, 'I'm gonna meet Gordon Monday night. We'll party hearty, huh?'"

"A drug deal?" Drew asked.

"No, he's going to buy party balloons. Of course a drug deal! What else would it be?

And the best part is, I know when and where!" Jinx grinned. "I'm pretty good at this, huh? Jinx Harris, master snoop!"

Drew stared at the sand at his feet.

"What are you thinking?" Jinx asked. Then he shook his head. "No don't tell me. It's bound to be too sensible. The meeting is set for Monday night at eight. And guess where? The Cary cottage!"

"I'm thinking we have to tell Sheriff Greenwood," Drew said.

"Aw, I told you not to tell me!" Jinx said. "And what good will that do, anyway? His mind's made up. The police already looked. They can't just take our word for it this time."

"My dad, then," Drew said. "He'll believe me."

"Yeah, right," Jinx said. "Your dad will believe us. But then what? You think he's going to let us try to catch an escaped convict? Think again. Look, this is our chance. We can do it!"

Drew didn't say anything.

"It's not like it's really dangerous or anything. We can fix it so Tommy Gordon never even sees us! And once we take his picture, Sheriff Greenwood will have to believe us," Jinx insisted. "Then he'll keep little Crash Gordon safe, and you'll be off the hook."

Drew thought about Josh, with all his annoying habits and his silly rooster tail hair.

"We'll need Allie," he said. "It's dark by eight. She'll know how we can get a picture. And I'll leave a note for my dad, just in case."

"Yes!" Jinx tried to high-five him, but Drew was staring out at the flat ledges off

North Point. Whitecaps dotted the water. The wind was picking up. This was the rockiest part of the shoreline. And beyond the rocks was deep water.

* * *

Jinx insisted they cut through backyards on the way to Allie's house. They peered into sheds and garages, looking for Tommy Gordon's sleeping place. That's what got them into trouble.

They were trying to see in the window of a tool shed. Drew edged sideways. He knocked over a metal trash can, and it fell with an ear-splitting crash.

"Who's out there?" A woman's raspy shout came from the side porch of the house. Drew recognized that voice.

"Whose house is this?" he whispered. But he already knew.

"You come out of there!" Mrs. Firbush

yelled, closer now. "You're trespassing!"

Drew opened his mouth to answer. But then Jinx was yanking him, hard, by the jacket. They stumbled under a clothesline and ran a few feet to the back of the house. Before Drew realized what Jinx was doing, he had opened the slanted door to the cellar. Drew felt himself pulled down rough, concrete stairs.

They crouched on the steps. Jinx lowered the door, all but half an inch. He propped it ajar with a Swiss army knife from his pocket. A strip of light fell across his face. He was smiling. He looked excited. In fact, he looked a little like Josh at his worst, Drew decided.

"What are you...?" Drew began.

"Shhh!" Jinx said. He pointed and they both looked out the open crack. Margaret Firbush was walking toward the shed. She passed out of sight.

They heard a metal rattle. Then Mrs. Firbush was back where they could see her. Margaret Firbush looked like a human dumpling. In the cafeteria, she always wore a uniform and a hair net over her screaming-red hair. Now she was dressed in pink Bermuda shorts, black tank top, and an open denim shirt. Drew really wished he had not seen her in this outfit.

The laundry on the clothesline was whipping in the wind. Mrs. Firbush started pulling clothespins off the line. She piled two pairs of pants and a man's blue shirt over her left arm.

Drew stared at the shirt. It reminded him of something. What?

Then he remembered.

He put his hand on Jinx's arm.

"What color was the shirt Mrs. Firbush said we took?"

"You got me." Jinx shrugged.

"What about that guy Josh said was his dad? He was wearing a blue shirt. I saw it when he was near the ferry dock." Drew started to stand up. "We've got to ask her."

Jinx pulled him back down. "Are you nuts?" he hissed. "She'll flatten us! We're in her cellar. She'll have us arrested!"

"All right. We'll get Liz to ask her."

"Or Owen," Jinx said. "It would serve him right."

Drew settled back down. He looked outside. Most of the wash was off the line. The wind blew a towel out of Mrs. Firbush's hands. She bent over to pick it up. Drew looked away.

"Jinx," Drew whispered. "You didn't put that scarecrow on the toilet on the front lawn at school. Did you?"

"Hey! Don't underestimate me," Jinx said. "I don't tell you everything." But Drew could hear a grin in Jinx's voice.

"She's taking a long time," Drew said.

"Yeah," Jinx agreed. Then he scrambled up onto his knees. "Holy moly! Look at this!" he said.

Drew put his eye to the opening. What he saw made him jerk back and bump his head on the door frame. Mrs. Firbush was walking toward the back door, a huge pile of clothes in her arms. The wind was ruffling everything, including her wild red hair. In fact, it was blowing her whole head of hair straight up, lifting it in a big clump. It was a wig. Underneath, Mrs. Firbush's bare head was smooth and shiny.

"Dibs!" Jinx whispered.

"Dibs? On what?" Drew asked.

"On that!" Jinx said. "It's perfect. It's the perfect Ragged Island secret!"

* * *

Josh's mom came running up Spruce Road first thing the next morning, Saturday. She must have taken the early ferry from Bellport. Drew and Josh were sitting on the front steps of Drew's house, eating oatmeal with peanut butter and banana slices. It was Josh's favorite.

Black smears of makeup smudged the pale skin under Darlene Gordon's eyes. She looked like she hadn't slept much.

She was breathing hard from running. She folded Josh in a big hug and buried her nose in his hair. "Snuggles!" she announced. "Double-heavy-duty snuggles!" Then she hugged him even harder.

She stood and looked at Drew, still clutching Josh in her arms.

"Oh, Drew." Her voice shook. "I don't even know what to say. I'm sorry." She smoothed Joshie's hair. The kid was way too big for her. She shifted him higher in her arms. "I was at a friend's apartment and I... I fell asleep. I can't believe I did that! I must have been really wiped out. By the time I woke up, it was the middle of the night. Too late to call, even. I feel really bad!"

She sounded scared—scared and very, very sorry. Her eyes had a pleading look in them.

Grown-ups didn't usually look at kids that way. It made Drew feel squirmy.

"I'm so sorry! Truly!" Darlene said. "It will never, ever happen again. And I really don't want you to quit."

She was waiting for him to say

something, Drew realized. But before he could answer, his mom came out on the front steps.

"Drew," she said. "You need to go pick up your room and make your bed."

He never made his bed.

"Right now," his mom said.

Drew ran up the steps and into the house. The screen door banged behind him. He knew his mom was about to give Darlene Gordon a piece of her mind.

Later in the morning, he helped his mom in the shelter. He held a beagle pup on his lap while she changed the bandage on the cut on its leg.

"Did you know Tommy Gordon?" he asked her.

She nodded. "Mmm."

"I guess he was really a rotten guy, huh?"

She didn't answer for a minute. "Well,"

she said, "he certainly did some rotten things." She spread fresh ointment on the pup. It squirmed in Drew's arms.

"But do you think he'd do something REALLY bad? Like stab somebody or something?"

Dr. Ellis stopped and looked up at him. "Drugs are really bad, Drew. They're terribly destructive." She wrapped the new bandage in neat overlaps. She reached for the tape. "But the truth is, I liked Tommy Gordon. He was funny. He cared about animals. Do I think he would be violent? Really hurt somebody?" She paused. "Not really. But I'm not going to bet my kid's well-being on it." She snipped the bandage and taped it. "So if you see him again, your dad or I had better hear about it right away. Got it?"

"Got it."

"And if there's one more episode with

Mrs. Gordon, you're going to have to quit that baby-sitting job. Understood?"

"How could she do that, Mom? Leave Josh like that?"

"Darned if I know." Dr. Ellis kissed the pup on the top of its head and plopped it into its cage. "People just mess up sometimes, I guess. Believe it or not, becoming a mother doesn't automatically make you perfect." She hugged Drew to her. "Although I can completely understand how YOU would think it does!"

"Huh?" Drew said.

But she just laughed.

* * * *

Allie agreed to watch the drug deal with Drew and try to get a picture.

"It'll be tricky," she said. "It's dark by eight o'clock. But I won't be able to use a flash. And I'll need a shutter release, maybe."

"You'll figure it out," Jinx said.

Allie had nodded. Drew could almost see the ideas churning in her head already.

That night as he was trying to fall asleep, Drew thought about Allie and her list of things a convict would need. Food. Clothes. Money. A place to sleep. A boat. It made a lot of sense. They were all things Tommy Gordon would need. But so far, none of them had led anywhere.

Drew turned over and punched his pillow. He remembered huddling with Jinx in the cellar and he smiled. His friends were the greatest.

Wait a minute... Friends.

Friends! Maybe that was it!

9

FOUND: ONE FRIEND

As soon as he got up the next morning,
Drew grabbed Allie's list and a pencil. He
wrote *Friends* at the top. Yes. That would
work. If Tommy Gordon had a friend helping
him, he would have a place to sleep. He
wouldn't need to find food. He wouldn't
even need a boat. Not if his friend had one.

But what about clothes? He might steal
them if his friend's clothes were too big or
too small.

Whatever. The friend idea worked. But who could it be?

Not Darlene Gordon. Drew was pretty sure of that. She had divorced Tommy, and she had told Drew she didn't want Tommy near Josh.

Drew got dressed and went to the kitchen. He threw a handful of cornflakes into his mouth while he thought.

Who else was there? Could Sheriff Greenwood be the friend? Maybe THAT'S why the police didn't find Tommy.

No. That was too far-fetched.

Drew racked his brain. Who? Who?

Lonnie Bickford? No. He didn't have a boat. And there would be no reason for Lonnie to set up a meeting with an escaped convict if he was already helping him, would there? No. Lonnie was out.

Old Mr. Dawson liked Tommy Gordon.

He'd said so at the diner that time. But Drew couldn't see Mr. Dawson helping an escaped convict.

Who else?

Wait. Mr. Dawson had said Tommy Gordon was friendly with someone. Drew closed his eyes and tried to remember. Mike! Mike Cappella! Mike Cappella, the nice guy. The lobster fisherman. And he had his own boat!

Drew thought for a minute. He yelled to tell his mom where he was going. Then he grabbed his disposable camera and headed out. He jumped on his bike and started coasting down Spruce Road.

"Hi, Drew."

Owen had appeared out of nowhere, on a bike way too small for him. His thick glasses glinted in the sun.

"What do you want, Owen?"

"I was waiting for you." They started up a hill lined with dark, sweet-smelling spruce trees. Owen's knees stuck up above the handlebars as he pedaled. "Where are we going?" he asked.

We?

"Accept it," Drew thought. "You're surrounded by pipsqueaks." But maybe this particular pipsqueak could be helpful this time. He told Owen the plan.

* * * *

Mike Cappella lived in a shake-covered house on Beach Road, down near Moody Head. An old pickup loaded with smelly bait barrels sat in the driveway. But no one answered Drew's knock.

"Over there, I think." Owen pointed toward Salt Creek, on the other side of the road. "I hear hammering."

He was right. Drew heard it now, too.

They tramped down the rough dirt track that led to the mouth of Salt Creek.

"Let me do the talking," Drew said.

It wasn't until then that he realized he didn't have a clue what he was going to say.

The road ended at a curve in Salt Creek. A lone lobster boat, neat and gleaming, was tied up to a small dock.

Owen squinted at the name on the stern. "What does it say?" he asked.

"*Island Pony*," Drew told him.

A man on the dock was repairing a lobster car, a wooden crate used for storing lobsters underwater. A few nails stuck out of his mouth. A baseball cap was pulled down, backward, over his head. A patch of shiny skin showed through the opening where you could adjust the hat size.

Drew started to explain that they were looking for interesting facts about Ragged

Island for a school project. He hoped Mike would jump in with a suggestion.

But Mike Cappella turned out to be the strong, silent type. Completely silent. He just kept hammering.

Drew's tongue felt like a brick. "So, uh, see, we thought maybe you could, uh..." COULD WHAT? He took a breath. "Um, since you know all about, well..."

"Oh, sure," he thought. "Since you know all about an escaped convict, could you please just tell me? So I can have you arrested?"

This would never work. What had he been thinking?

Mike Cappella just looked at him.

"And on Ragged Island lobstering is, well...important. And we were just wondering..."

"I GOTTA GO," Owen interrupted.

He was leaving? Now? "Okay," Drew said. He turned back to Mike.

"No," said Owen. "I mean, I gotta GO! Now!" He stepped closer to the man on the dock. "Is that your house over there, mister?" he asked. "Could I...use your bathroom?"

The kid was brilliant!

Drew watched, amazed, as Mike Cappella

finally gave a short nod. The man led the boys back up the road.

Once inside the house, Owen followed Mike Cappella's pointing finger. He bumped his shoulder against the door and then disappeared into the bathroom.

Drew and Owen had agreed the kitchen and the bathroom were the two best rooms in which to look for clues. They wanted to see if someone besides Mike was around. Maybe there would be two places set at the table or something. Then they'd know that Tommy Gordon was living there.

"Can I have a drink of water?" Drew asked.

Mike Cappella tilted his head and looked at him suspiciously. But finally he said, "Okay." He headed for a doorway. Drew followed.

The kitchen was utterly neat. Not a

spoon sat on the counter. Not a crumb on the table. Drew tried not to let his disappointment show. He accepted a giant glass of water. Too bad he wasn't thirsty.

Then Owen came back. Drew knew right away he'd found something. Owen kept mouthing "YES!" and making his eyes big. He gave a slow, obvious wink when he thought Mike wasn't looking. Drew wished he could jam a paper bag over Owen's head.

Instead, he thanked Mike Cappella and hustled Owen out the door.

As soon as they were outside, Owen broke the news. "He's there!" he said. "He's definitely there!"

"Shh!" Drew said. "Come on!"

Liz was waiting when they got back to Drew's house. She came running.

"Blue!" she said. "The shirt he stole from Mrs. Firbush was blue!"

"Bingo!" Drew said. He filled her in on where they'd been. Then he turned to Owen. "Now, tell!" he said.

Owen nodded.

"Well, it was on the sink," he said. "There was mouthwash, a razor, and a comb. Nothing special. But then I saw it! It was so obvious!"

"What?" Liz looked like she was going to shake him. "What?"

"It was a cup. And in it were two toothbrushes!"

"And...?" Liz said.

"And that's it!" Owen answered.

"That's what?"

"Two toothbrushes!" Owen said. "If only one person lives there, why are there two toothbrushes? One has to be Tommy's!"

"Oh, Owen." Liz plopped down on the grass. "Two toothbrushes is nothing. I have two toothbrushes. I use one in the morning and one at night. My dentist says...oh, it doesn't matter. But anybody can have two toothbrushes. That doesn't mean a thing."

Owen looked like a balloon with a slow leak.

But Drew was looking thoughtful. "Owen," he said, "tell me again what was on the sink."

Owen frowned. "Mouthwash," he said. "The green kind. And a disposable razor. And a comb."

Drew smiled. "Double bingo," he said.

115

"What would Mike Cappella need a comb for? He's completely bald!"

10

FACE TO FACE

Drew was sure now. Tommy Gordon was on Ragged Island.

What he didn't expect was to run into Tommy face to face.

It was Monday, Josh's day with his grandparents. Drew was on his way home from dinner at the diner.

A man stood beside a stand of sumac along the Ellis driveway. The sun was going down. His face was in shadow. But Drew knew it was Tommy. He knew it even before he got close enough to see the teardrop tattoo at the corner of his eye.

Drew's heart was pounding. His brain told him, "RUN! YELL FOR HELP!" But he didn't. He just had to know. He had to know what Tommy Gordon wanted. He walked within about twenty feet of the man and stopped.

Tommy Gordon was thin, and only a couple of inches taller than Drew. Drew had assumed he'd be bigger. Tommy Gordon's black hair was shaggy and too long. But his shirt—blue with rolled-up sleeves—was clean and tucked neatly into his jeans.

Tommy Gordon smiled. He put both hands up, palms out. "It's okay," he said. "Drew. Right?"

Drew nodded.

"You know who I am?" Tommy Gordon took a step closer.

Drew nodded again.

"Drew, I need to talk to you about Josh."
The man's voice was quiet, gentle. He was
trying not to sound scary. Drew could tell.

"You see, I gotta take him."

Tommy Gordon stepped forward again.

Drew took a step back.

"I watched you with him," Gordon said. "You like him, right?"

Drew didn't answer.

"Well, it's like this, Drew. I'm taking Josh with me. You can make it easy, or you can make it hard. It's up to you."

Drew felt a hot blast of anger roll through his chest. He forgot he was just a kid. "Don't you hurt Josh!" he burst out. His voice cracked, but he kept going. "He's a little boy. He didn't do it on purpose. He didn't know he'd get you sent to jail. And if you touch him, I'll...I'll..."

Drew didn't know what he'd do. Before he could decide, he realized Tommy Gordon was laughing. Laughing!

The man wiped his eyes on his shirt sleeve. "Is that what you thought?" He shook his head. "You got it all wrong, kid. Joshie's my son. I love every hair on that boy's head." His voice sounded fierce. "I'm taking him away from here. I'm his daddy. I got a right."

He was so angry—so desperate. How was a kid like Drew going to keep Josh from this man?

As soon as he thought it, the answer came. "My camera," Drew remembered.

He had his disposable camera with him. He took it everywhere now. If he had a picture, the adults would help. He had to keep Tommy Gordon talking.

"What do you want me to do?" he asked. He snaked his right hand around to the back pocket of his jeans. He tried to make it a casual move.

"Josh will come with me, no problem," Tommy Gordon said. "I could have grabbed him a few times now. But you might have fought me. And I don't want him upset. I don't want him confused. I'm here to tell you —you just gotta let him go. He's in a bad situation here. I'm taking him with me."

The camera was stuck tight in Drew's pocket. He tried to work it loose.

"What bad situation?"

Tommy Gordon didn't say anything for a moment. He looked like he was trying to make a decision.

Then he shook his head. "Yeah, okay," he said. "I did a few things I'm not proud of. I'm not saying I didn't break the law sometimes. But selling the cocaine? Nah."

"Tommy Good-Heart," Drew thought. "Right. Tell me another one." He had wiggled the camera up to the top of his pocket. Almost there. Then it slipped over the top edge and fell down the back of his leg to the ground. Had Tommy Gordon seen it? Heard it? Drew couldn't tell.

"The drugs, that wasn't me, see?" Tommy Gordon was saying. "Darlene. She's the one."

"Don't listen to him," Drew told himself. "He's a convict. He's trying to trick you. He'll say anything to get what he wants. The guy has a drug deal on for this very night!"

Gordon was still talking. "Darlene grew up here. She went to school on this island. So who's going to believe ME, huh?" Gordon shook his head. He ran a hand through his hair.

"Darlene's still dealing drugs. Using, too. She promised me she'd stop." Gordon's right hand made a fist. "She's still getting high. What kind of a mother is that?" He took a deep breath. "So I'm taking my kid out of here."

He sounded so believable. And if he was telling the truth, it would explain some

123

things about Darlene Gordon. But criminals lied. They couldn't be trusted.

"You're on the run from the police," Drew said. "You can't do that to Josh." He edged one foot back until it touched the camera. He tensed up and got ready to grab for it. "What kind of life is that for a little kid?"

Tommy Gordon's face got a set look, like he'd heard that before. "He's my son. I'll take care of him. You just remember. You'll only make it harder for Josh if you fight me over him."

He came closer. He was a small man, but the muscles in his forearms were hard and bunched.

"Now step back, Drew," Tommy said.

Drew took a small backwards step.

"More. Move way back."

Drew moved back until the camera was

lying exposed in the dirt between them. Tommy Gordon stepped forward quickly. He stomped on the plastic camera case. Once. Twice. Then he took off through the bushes.

11

I Want My Daddy

It was time to have a little talk with his parents, Drew decided. Past time, even. He imagined the conversation: "Excuse me, Mom and Dad, but an escaped convict followed me home. Can I keep him?" Oh, boy.

But when Drew got home, the house was empty. He'd forgotten. It was Monday—his mom's night at the Bellport clinic.

Jinx and Liz weren't going to the stakeout. It was Mrs. French's birthday.

The whole family was going out to dinner on the mainland.

That left Allie. Drew tried to call to tell her what was up. The line was busy. He looked at his watch. It was 6:25. The meeting between Lonnie Bickford and Tommy Gordon was set for 8:00. He was supposed to meet Allie at the Cary cottage at 7:30. That meant he still had time to get help.

The plan was for Allie to wedge her camera into a tree or a bush with its wide-angle lens pointed at the cottage. Allie had equipped the camera with a super-long shutter release. It was like a bulb on a long cord. When you squeezed the bulb, the camera took a picture. They could set up the camera close to the cottage and stay much farther back themselves, hiding.

Of course, there was still the chance Lonnie and Tommy might hear the camera click. And if they did, they would NOT be happy. But while they went for the camera, Drew and Allie would run. If they were back far enough, they would have a good head start.

Drew hoped they wouldn't need that head start. Tommy Gordon had a lot to lose.

It was still dinnertime at the diner. Drew's dad would be up to his chin in meatloaf and chowder. Drew picked up the phone and called the Animal Night Clinic in Bellport.

"I'm sorry, Drew." the lab assistant said. "Dr. Ellis is in surgery. A collie chased a seagull out into the street down by the wharf and got hit by a car. He's hurt pretty bad, poor old guy. Can I give her a message?"

It looked like he'd have to bother his dad after all. Drew put down the phone and sprinted for his bike.

When he got to the diner, the supper rush was in full swing.

"Drew! Thank goodness! Here! Take these to Booth 3." Sharon shoved two plates at him and disappeared into the kitchen.

Great. Now, instead of staking out a drug deal, he was delivering hot turkey sandwiches to his dentist and her husband.

Drew topped off everybody's coffee on Sharon's orders. Then he made his way to the kitchen. He still didn't see his dad.

"He's not here, hon." Sharon pushed past him to reach for a gallon container of mustard. "He had one of those small business owners' meetings. He won't be back until about ten. Those meetings go on forever."

Drew took a deep breath. He would just have to figure out something else.

Okay. All right. What now?

"You know what now," he told himself. "You have to do it. You have to call the sheriff, even if he does think you're a wacko kid with an overactive imagination. You have to." He looked at his watch.

No! Oh, no!

His watch said 6:25...6:25, just like before. How long had it been stopped before he checked it the first time?

Drew practically dived through the kitchen door to the front of the diner. "Please!" he thought. "Please!"

He looked at the clock over the counter. 7:45.

Allie! Allie was already at the Cary cottage, all alone.

Drew panicked. He started for Maine Street at a run. Then he stopped himself. The cottage wasn't far. But it would take a few minutes to get there. What if Lonnie or

Tommy saw him? He'd ruin everything. Not only that. He might put Allie in danger.

Allie had a level head, that was for sure. She'd know by now he wasn't coming. She might decide it was too dangerous to go through with it on her own, and she'd get out of there.

"No. Be honest with yourself," Drew thought. "She'll do it. She'll do it all by herself. And she's probably really scared.

"Oh, Allie! I'm sorry!"

* * *

Drew sat on the sofa at home and stared at the blank TV screen. He kept imagining Allie. "She got the pictures, she retrieved the camera, and she went on home," he told himself. No problem. After all, spying on the drug deal was no more dangerous now than it had been when they first thought of it. It was just that now he had seen Tommy

Gordon face to face. It seemed more REAL somehow.

He'd been sitting there a long time. He wished Allie would call. But he doubted she'd have a chance, not this late on a school night.

He didn't want to think any more—not about what he was going to say to his dad, and not about what Tommy Gordon had told him. But he couldn't help it. He thought about how Josh got left overnight. He remembered how Joshie wore the same T-shirts day after day and how there was never milk in his house.

But Darlene Gordon loved Joshie. Drew knew it. Moms are good, he told himself. Prison convicts are bad. That's all. The end. He shouldn't have to figure it out any further than that. No. Let the grown-ups deal with it. All he had to do now was to stay awake until his dad got home.

Drew yawned. He imagined Allie walking through her front door, putting down her camera, and saying goodnight. He replayed it over and over in his mind. If he imagined it enough, then it had to be true.

* * * *

When he woke up, the morning sun was warm on his face, and he was covered with a blanket. His dad had already left for work again. And he was late for school. Oh, man!

Drew practically flew to the school office and then to first period English. There she was! Allie was in her regular seat. She looked just the same. No gunshot wounds. No missing limbs. Drew stared a question at her. She nodded her head.

So she'd gotten a picture! Yes! Now all they had to do was show it to the sheriff. The police could stake out Mike Cappella's house—and his boat, maybe. Then they would take Tommy Gordon back to prison. Of course, neither Drew nor Allie would be around to see it. Once their parents found out what they'd been doing, they'd both be grounded until they were thirty.

* * * *

"Look what I made, Drew!"

Josh crashed into him from behind. It was their usual after-school collision. This time Josh was pulling something out of his backpack.

"It's all for you!" he yelled.

It was a drawing. At the top, Josh's teacher had carefully printed *My Family*. On one side of the paper, on a ferry boat in a puddle of water, was a small female stick figure with bright red lips. That was Darlene, obviously. On the other side, in a rocket ship, was another stick figure. Tommy? And in the middle, biggest of all, were the Drew and Josh figures, holding hands. Josh only came up to about Drew's knees.

"I look so big and powerful," Drew thought. "Oh, man."

"Who's that?" he asked. He pointed to an orange splot in the corner of the page. It was surrounded by a brown smear.

"That's my dead goldfish," Josh said. "Mrs. Halter said to put pets in, too."

Jinx strolled up and looked over Drew's shoulder. Allie and Owen were standing behind him.

"What happened last night?" Allie asked Drew.

Drew shook his head. "It's a long story. I've got some stuff to tell you guys. I'm really sorry, Allie! Are you all right?"

"Sure," Allie said.

"They didn't see you?"

"No way. In fact, I couldn't even see THEM. I hid behind that wooden screen beside the wood pile. The dog next door must have known I was there, though. He never quit barking. I think that's why they didn't hear the camera clicking."

Drew nodded. "How did the pictures come out?"

"What pictures?" Josh asked. "Can I see them? Can I? Can I?" He jumped up and down. Jinx yelped and grabbed his foot.

Allie shrugged. "I didn't have time to develop them last night. I thought I'd do that right now. Meet me back here in about an hour?"

"I'll go with you, Allie," Jinx said, "before Crash cripples me for life." They took off. Jinx was limping.

"Hey! Where's Liz?" Drew shouted after them.

Jinx waved a hand toward the school doors. "In there somewhere."

A few kids were still straggling out of the building. One or two teachers were beginning to drive out of the parking lot. Drew planned to stay near a lot of people, then enlist all his friends to help walk Josh to the diner. Then they could get some help from his dad.

Josh and Owen started playing a weird version of blind man's bluff. Drew set his backpack down and watched. First Owen put his glasses on Joshie's nose. Then they took turns hiding around the giant jungle gym. Owen was practically blind without his glasses. Josh could barely see through their thick lenses, and his backpack drooped heavily off his skinny shoulders. They did a lot of stumbling around and bumping into things. Both of them seemed to find this game very funny.

Drew sat on the grass near the stone wall that bordered the playground. He felt like he was stumbling around too. Was Tommy Gordon telling the truth? If so, he was innocent, and Josh's mother was the real criminal. Could that be? Sometimes Drew didn't like the way Mrs. Gordon acted with Joshie. But he could tell she loved the kid. And Josh loved her. Of course, Josh seemed to adore his father too. But even so, would it be right to let him go live with a criminal? WERE you a criminal if you really didn't do anything? Oh, this was all too hard.

And Drew had daydreamed too long. When he looked up, Owen and Josh were the only two people around. Correction. The only two except for himself and Tommy Gordon. Josh's father was walking toward him from the path to the playing fields. He stopped a few feet away.

"Now or never, Drew," Tommy Gordon said in his quiet voice. "Are you gonna help me?"

Drew looked over at Joshie. He was staggering along the tire maze. He hadn't seen his father yet.

"This isn't right!" Drew said.

"I'll take good care of him," Tommy said.

"Can't you just tell them that Mrs. Gordon did it?" Drew whispered. "I know. You can tell her she has to stop doing drugs. Otherwise you'll tell on her."

"Who'd believe me? I'd need proof. And I don't have any." Tommy Gordon started for Josh. "This is the only way."

"No! I can't let you. I'm sorry! I can't!" Drew ran past him and grabbed Josh around the waist.

"Don't do this, kid," Tommy Gordon said.

"Come on with me, Josh." Drew pushed Josh's backpack up higher on his back and started hustling him toward the school. But it was too late. Josh twisted to look back, and Owen's glasses fell off his nose.

"Daddy! You came!"

Josh's father smiled. "I told you I would," he said.

Josh wiggled. "Let me go, Drew. It's my dad."

Drew held tighter. He tried to walk to the school, but Josh was squirming too much. "Hey, let go!" Josh said.

Tommy Gordon came closer.

"Owen!" Drew cried. "Go get help!"

"Okay!" Owen said. But he was down on his knees, feeling around on the ground for his glasses. He'd never get help in time.

"This isn't going to do any good," Tommy said. "Let him go." His hand closed on Drew's arm. It was hard and strong. He was going to get Josh, and there was nothing Drew could do.

"Are we going on the pony, Daddy?" Josh asked.

"You bet. I said so, didn't I?" Tommy Gordon pulled one of Drew's arms away.

Then Drew saw something out of the

corner of his eye. A car! A gray sedan was nosing out of the teachers' lot, just past a line of bushes.

Tommy Gordon saw it too. He pushed Drew to the side. He tried to pick his son up. But Drew threw both arms back around Josh.

"Mrs. Lord!" he yelled. He could just see the teacher's face behind the wheel. "Mrs. Lord! Over here!"

The car came closer. It slowed.

The look on Tommy Gordon's face was scary. He took Josh's face between his hands. "Don't forget the pony," he said. "Promise."

Josh started to cry. "Take me there now, Daddy. Please!"

"I can't, Josh." Tommy Gordon was already backing away. "Soon. Don't worry. I love you!" He started running. He tripped.

143

Then he got up and kept going.

"I'll meet you there!" Josh was sobbing now. He twisted in Drew's arms. He kicked at Drew's shins. "Daddy!" he shrieked. "I want my dad!" He elbowed Drew in the chest. "Let me go! Drew! Please! He's a good guy. DADDY!" His elbow got Drew in the face this time. Drew jerked back and Josh wiggled out of his grasp. He started to run. But Drew lunged and grabbed him again by the shirt.

"Let me go! I hate you. I hate you!" Josh was hitting and kicking with all his might.

The car had rolled right on by. Mrs. Lord hadn't even seen them. Drew shivered.

He started toward the school, Josh in tow. But after just two steps, he bumped right into Owen. They both went down. That gave Josh his chance. He pulled out of Drew's grasp and took off toward the soccer field.

Drew lurched up and grabbed for him. He slipped on the grass. He went down to his knees again. He was pushing back up and already after Josh again when he saw Jinx and Allie jogging in from the road.

"Over here!" he shouted.

Josh saw them too. He swerved and ran toward the school doors, his heavy backpack banging against him with each step.

"What happened?" Jinx grabbed Drew's arm.

"Tommy Gordon happened," Drew said. "Did you see where Josh went?"

"It's okay," Allie said. "When he saw us coming, he turned around and went into the school. Come on."

She handed Drew two photos. "Look at these on the way."

The photos were dark. The figures were blurred. But Drew could make out the bulky shape of Lonnie Bickford. And he could see the figure next to Lonnie, too. Drew stopped short at the top of the school steps. The person was small and slight. Clearly, it was a woman.

"The oaf said he was meeting Gordon," Jinx said. "I just assumed he meant Tommy. But it was DARLENE Gordon he went to meet. Duh! It must not have been drugs after all. I never even thought of her."

"Sorry they're no help," Allie said.

Oh, these photos were a help, all right. A big help. Drew thought about the notebook he had seen in Josh's backpack. Now he knew what all those numbers were. He started to tell Allie, then stopped. How would it affect Josh if everyone knew? It was not his secret to tell, Drew decided. At least, not yet.

Just then, the door of the school swung wide. Liz burst out.

"Drew?" she shouted. "I think I just saw Josh take off out the back doors."

They searched the whole school. Josh was gone. Liz ran for the Gordon house, to make sure he hadn't gone home. The rest of them argued about where else to look.

"He went to meet his father," Jinx said.

"Yes. But where?" said Drew.

"Maybe the Cary cottage?" Allie asked. "His dad was there before."

"Yeah. But I don't think Josh knew that." Drew was pacing. Now he knew what people meant when they said they were so frustrated they could pull their hair out. "They talked about a pony. Josh mentioned a pony before, too. When he got that phone call."

"Who has a pony on the island?" Jinx asked.

"The Millers?" Allie suggested.

"Yeah!" said Jinx. "Let's go!"

"No. This doesn't make sense," Drew insisted. "Tommy Gordon's on the run. Why would they be riding on a pony?"

Owen had been sitting on the floor, staring out the window. Now he spoke up. "Do you think it could be the *Island Pony*?"

"What?" Drew demanded.

"You know. *Island Pony*. Mike Cappella's boat."

The boat. Of course.

12

SAVING JOSH

Drew sent Owen into the school office to call the police station.

"They might not believe him," he told Jinx and Allie. "Allie, go down there. Don't give up until you get Sheriff Greenwood to Moody Head. Jinx, once Owen gets off the phone, call my dad, okay?"

"What about you?" Jinx asked.

"I'll borrow a bike and ride to the Head. If I can catch them, I think I know how to stop Tommy."

"That's too dangerous!" Allie cried. "He's an escaped convict! He's already stolen a kid. Aren't you scared?"

Drew shook his head. Tommy Gordon could have hurt him before. He didn't. "Josh says he's a good guy."

The look on Jinx's face should have made Drew laugh. But he didn't have time.

He stuck the photos in his backpack and jumped on the only bike left in the rack. It had a rusty chain and a pink basket on the front. "I'll bring it back," he promised the owner silently. Then he pedaled until his lungs felt like they were on fire.

The track to Salt Creek was too sandy for the bike. Drew dumped it. He thought he saw a window shade being pulled at the Cappella house, but he wasn't sure. He ran.

It was still there! The *Island Pony* was still there. But barely. The engine was running.

Tommy Gordon was up on the bow, casting off the lines.

Drew ran across the dock. He took a flying leap. He landed with a WHUMP! on the boat's deck.

"Drew!" Josh was standing on a box, turning the steering wheel back and forth. "Look! I'm the captain!" His face was still tear-streaked, but he was grinning. It was as if the hassle at the school had never happened. The backpack was still on his back. Drew took a deep breath. He could still do it. He could still keep Josh safe. He crossed the deck and gave the kid a hug, backpack and all.

Tommy Gordon swung back onto the deck then. He didn't act surprised to see Drew. He just looked at him and waited.

"Can I get something out of your pack, Josh?" Drew asked. He opened the backpack. He pulled out the notebook. Then he took the photos out of his own pack.

"You have it," he said to Tommy Gordon. "Look. You have the proof you need." He held them out.

Tommy looked at the photos. He flipped though the notebook. He nodded. Then he stuffed them all in Josh's backpack.

"You're a good kid," he said. "Yeah. Thanks. But you're too late."

"What?" Drew couldn't believe it.

"We're going. Josh and me."

"But that notebook has all the drug deals in it! All those numbers and initials! They're the people she sold drugs to. And the money she made!"

But Tommy was watching Joshie. The kid was having a great time, climbing all over the boat. Josh lay down on the edge of the gunwale—the ledge on the boat's side—and

dragged one hand in the water.

"Get down from there, son," Tommy Gordon said. He turned to Drew.

"I appreciate what you're saying, Drew, but I've got my kid now. We'll make a new life. We'll change our name."

"But don't you see? You can use this!" Drew said. "You can prove who really did it. You can have her arrested! Or you can force her to stop! If you show the notebook, everyone will know."

"That doesn't prove I didn't help her." Tommy shook his head. "Look, I'm not exactly pure as the driven snow myself. You know? And I'm an escapee. They don't let you off easy for that. And you don't know what it's like. I can't stand going back. No. Josh and I will take our chances."

"Get off the boat, Drew." He grabbed a dock support and pulled the boat close. The boat tipped down, then up. There was a yelp and a loud splash.

"Joshie!" Drew yelled. Josh had slipped off the other side.

At the same moment, a siren shrieked. The island's one police car was barreling down the track toward them. Drew could see his dad in the passenger seat.

Drew didn't even think. He tore off his pack and jacket.

He could see Josh in the water, kicking his feet and flailing his arms wildly. That backpack was heavy. It would drag him down.

"I'll get him!" Drew yelled. I'm a strong swimmer. You go!"

But Tommy Gordon had already made his choice. He disappeared over the side, a

155

clean slice into the cold water. A moment later, his head bobbed up. He looked around for Josh. Two strokes, and Tommy grabbed the frightened boy. He ripped the heavy pack from Josh's shoulders. Then he looked back at Drew. His eyes looked flat and hopeless.

Drew watched the soaked backpack sink like a stone.

"I'll testify for you!" he shouted. "I will! I promise!"

But Drew never knew for sure if Tommy Gordon heard him.

The next thing he knew, Sheriff Greenwood was hauling the escaped convict and his son out of the water. And Jim Ellis was hauling his son in for a big bear hug.

AFTERWORD

"What did the maple syrup say when it saw what Drew cooked?" Jinx asked.

"What?" said Liz and Allie together.

"What?" asked Owen.

"'Oh! How waffle!'"

Allie smiled and Liz groaned. They had to write it on a napkin for Owen. Then he got it and laughed like crazy.

The Fearsome Foursome was back at Mel's diner. Owen, too.

Drew's baby-sitting job was over, so he had decided to try working in the diner's kitchen. Just for a couple of weeks, until the last of the tourists went home. He figured if he could face down an escaped convict, he could take a little yelling with the burgers and fries.

Drew came out from behind the counter.

He plopped a giant super-duper hot fudge sundae onto the table at his friends' booth. They had all chipped in to buy it for Owen.

It was a celebration.

Owen had won a ribbon for the best Ragged Island secret in the whole school. He had written about Tommy Gordon and how they had found him. He had printed it out on a computer. It looked just like a real newspaper story.

Of course, it wasn't the whole story.

Only Drew knew that.

It turned out that Drew didn't need to testify. Tommy didn't need the notebook, either. Soon after Tommy Gordon went back to jail, Darlene had checked herself into a drug rehabilitation place in Portland.

Tommy Gordon had gotten what he wanted. Drew was sure Tommy had written to Darlene. He must have told her he had the notebook. He must have said he'd show it to the police if she didn't stop using drugs.

That was blackmail. But it was for a good cause.

While his mom was "away" at the rehab place, Josh was living with his grandparents on their farm in Connecticut. He was probably annoying some poor, innocent horse at this very minute.

Drew missed him.

"Hey!" Allie pulled Drew into the seat beside her. "Don't I get a sundae too?"

Allie had won runner-up in the contest. She had taken pictures of her favorite "secret places" on Ragged Island. They were beautiful.

Jinx pulled a little gift bag out of his shirt pocket and set it in front of her. In it were two new rolls of film.

Jinx's secret had teachers giving him

funny looks. It was about how many cellar doors on the island were left unlocked. He even passed out pamphlets from the Portland police about how to avoid burglaries—with a straight face!

He never told about Mrs. Firbush's wig. When Drew asked about it, Jinx said he'd decided that it was boring. He would never admit he was being kind.

Liz hadn't told about any pranks, either. She said she was keeping the ideas to herself, just in case. Instead, she told how much ketchup and mustard kids ate in the school cafeteria every year. It was gallons— enough to make you feel very queasy.

And Drew? Well, he'd forgotten all about the project. He hadn't turned in a thing. For make-up work, he had to help Mrs. Lord display all the facts and secrets on giant sheets of paper in the school halls.

He didn't mind. Drew knew he had a secret that was bigger than any of them. But he would never tell. He was still watching out for Josh.

ABOUT THE AUTHOR

Deborah Eaton has written more than one hundred stories and books for young readers. Although she has slept many nights with the lights on after reading a scary mystery, *Watching Josh* is the first she's written. She loves to garden but has yet to outwit Chuck the Greedy-Guts, the woodchuck who lives under her garage. Deborah lives in a small town in Maine with her high-maintenance cat, Pudge.